Grandma Drove the Snowplow

Written by
Katie Clark

Illustrated by
Amy Huntington

ISBN 978-0-89272-851-0

Printed in China
2 4 5 3 1

Library of Congress
Cataloging-in-Publication Data
available on request

To Rob and Geoffrey
— K.C.

Thanks to the folks at Williston Public Works,
and to Martha, Harly, and Baby.
— A.H.

Brreep!

"Billy," said Grandma. "Check the cookies."
Billy looked in the oven.

Brreep!

But the cookies weren't ready.
It wasn't the oven timer.

Brreep!

It was the radio, with an emergency broadcast
announcement! Grandma turned up the volume:

Warning! The storm has changed direction.
Blizzard conditions are sweeping across the state.
18 to 24 inches of snow expected by nightfall.

"Oh, no!" said Billy. "But tonight's the Carol Sing!"

Grandma looked at the tins of cookies stacked on the counter and the basket of mittens all set to go by the door. "Don't you worry," she said. "We'll be fine, just fine. Buster's out in his truck. He'll get the roads cleared. He can plow through anything." She rolled out another lump of dough.

Now, in the summer Grandma ran the garbage business. Her three sons drove the trucks. But in the winter, when all the summer folks were gone, there just wasn't that much garbage. But there was always plenty of snow. So in the winter Grandma ran a snowplowing business, too.

And for everyone in town there was no bigger winter celebration than the Carol Sing. Starting the day after Thanksgiving people baked cookies, practiced songs, and knit pairs and pairs of mittens for the mitten tree. They hadn't missed a Carol Sing for as long as anyone could remember.

Rrring!

"Billy," said Grandma. "Are those cookies done?"

Rrring!

Billy checked the oven.

Rrring!

But it wasn't the oven timer. It was the telephone!

"Hello?" said Grandma.

"Oh, no," said Grandma.

"I see," said Grandma and she hung up the phone.

"Buster's stuck in a snow bank. He can't move forward. He can't move backward. And he certainly can't plow the roads in time for the Carol Sing."

"But," said Billy, "it starts in two hours!"

"Don't you worry," said Grandma. "We'll be fine, just fine. Burt's out in his truck, too. He'll get the roads cleared. He can plow through anything."

She slid another tray of cookies into the oven.

> *Rrring!*
>
> *Rrring!*
>
> *Rrring!*

Grandma looked at Billy. And Billy looked at Grandma. Then they both looked at the phone. They knew it wasn't the oven timer.

"Hello?" said Grandma.

"Oh, no," said Grandma.

"I see," said Grandma and she hung up the phone.

"Burt's stuck in a ditch. He can't move forward. He can't move backward.
And he certainly can't plow the roads in time for the Carol Sing."

"But," said Billy, "who's going to plow now?"

Grandma squinted across the room.

There sat Bill, her third and last son. He didn't need to say a thing.
They all knew there was no way he could drive a truck, much less
operate the snowplow.

"Terrible," said Grandma. "Just terrible, making folks miss the best party
of the season." Then she looked at her littlest grandson. But he didn't look
sad. He looked happy. And what was that he was holding in his hand?

"Come on, Grandma," said Billy. "Come on!
We've got a job to do. A BIG JOB!"

Grandma yanked off her apron and tossed the spatula
to Bill. "Don't let the last batch of cookies burn," she said.

Then she grabbed her coat.

Billy scooted into the front seat.

Grandma switched on the flashing lights. "If I can drive a garbage truck, I guess I can drive this ol' monster!"

She lowered the plow and barreled down the driveway.

"The wreath! The wreath!" cried Billy.

But Grandma didn't see. The wipers were beating

thwappity-thunk thwappity-thunk!

The snowplow churned around the corner.

"Let's just give these folks a hand," said Grandma.

"The reindeer! The reindeer!" shouted Billy.

But Grandma didn't hear. The wind was howling

Wheee-whooo Wheee-whooo Whooo!

The snowplow rumbled down the lane.

"Looks like the skaters could use our help," said Grandma.

"The tree! The tree!" yelled Billy.

But Grandma didn't notice. The snow was swirling

whoosh-swoosh
whoosh-swoosh!

The snowplow swerved onto Main Street.

Grandma put on her high beams.

She beeped her horn all the way to the front door of the church.

Roy Hardy grabbed the wreath.

Edna Fillmore strung up the lights.

And little Maggie Wells helped hang mittens on the tree.

"Merry Christmas, everyone!" hollered Grandma.

But Billy didn't look happy. He looked sad. "Where is he?" he said.

"Ho! Ho! Ho! Here I am!" Santa stomped snow from his boots. "That sure is some blizzard out there!"

Billy sat on Santa's lap.

He opened his present. Then he pulled something out of his pocket.

"This is for you," he said. "I knew you'd make it. You always do!"